THE MYTHICS

HAILEY AND THE DRAGON

LAUREN MAGAZINER
ILLUSTRATED BY MIRELLE ORTEGA

KATHERINE TEGEN BOOKS
An Imprint of HarperCollins Publishers

Katherine Tegen Books is an imprint of HarperCollins Publishers.

The Mythics #2: Hailey and the Dragon
Text copyright © 2023 by Lauren Magaziner
Illustrations copyright © 2023 by Mirelle Ortega

Library of Congress Cataloging-in-Publication Data
Names: Magaziner, Lauren, author. | Ortega, Mirelle, illustrator.
Title: Hailey and the dragon / by Lauren Magaziner;
    with illustrations by Mirelle Ortega.
Description: First edition. | New York, NY : Katherine Tegen
    Books, an imprint of HarperCollinsPublishers, [2023] | Series:
    The Mythics ; #2 | Audience: Ages 8-12. | Audience: Grades 4-6.
    | Summary: When Hailey and her four fellow Mythics set out
    to find her mythical beast familiar and fight a powerful villain
    along the way, she realizes what it means to be part of a team.
Identifiers: LCCN 2022031708 | ISBN 9780063058927 (hardcover)
Subjects: CYAC: Mythical animals--Fiction. | Familiars
    (Spirits)--Fiction. | Dragons--Fiction. | Daredevils--Fiction. |
    Cooperativeness--Fiction. | LCGFT: Fantasy fiction. | Novels.
Classification: LCC PZ7.M2713 Hai 2023 | DDC [Fic]--dc23
LC record available at https://lccn.loc.gov/2022031708

Typography by Laura Mock
23 24 25 26 27 LBC 5 4 3 2 1

First Edition

To Tae Keller and Booki Vivat—
My brave, brilliant writer squad.
I'm so fortunate to experience the magic
of your friendship.

TERRAFAMILIAR

LAVASIDE
ROCKS

MOUNTAINSIDE
SNOWS

SPLASHSIDE FALLS

SEASIDE
SANDS

TUNDRASIDE
FROSTS

WOODSIDE
TIMBERS

PRAIRIESIDE
MEADOWS

RIVERSIDE
REEDS

CLIFFSIDE
LEDGES

SAVANNASIDE
GRASSES

SWAMPSIDE
SHRUBS

DESERTSIDE
DUNES

JUNGLESIDE
VINES

LAKESIDE
MUDS

N

WATERSIDE
ISLES

W

E

S

1

PATIENCE

Hailey couldn't wait. She paced back and forth on top of the rock, buzzing with excitement. She looked behind her. Her friends were partway down the mountain, very small in the distance.

"Hurry up! Hurry up! Faster!" Hailey shouted to Pippa, Ember, Marina, and Kit.

They were taking FOREVER.

But then again, most things felt like FOREVER to Hailey. The perfect example? Pairing Day. The biggest, bestest, most special day of Hailey's life was only two weeks ago, but it felt like a million years had passed since then.

Pairing Day was the greatest day ever, but not for the reason she thought it'd be. She had been so excited because she was *so sure* she'd get an animal to match her hyper, adventurous spirit—like a flying squirrel or a lemur or a hummingbird or a kangaroo.

But then no animal ever came. For her or for Ember. After that, there was a flurry of activity, and she had to fly across the world with her family, Ember and her moms, and Mayor Verioldman in a basket flown by condors and eagles—the familiars of the people who ran Soaring Sky Travel Service. Because everyone knew that familiar-travel was faster than any other type of travel.

When she arrived at Seaside Sands, she saw the

east ocean for the first time. Then she'd met Pippa, who came from Lakeside Muds. Finally, she'd met Kit and Marina. That's when the awesome thing happened—when they all put their hands in together, their palms started glowing and arrows appeared, and they suddenly got a mission to find their mythical beast familiars.

At that moment, Hailey realized that she was *destined* for adventure. Just like she always dreamed.

Because she was a MYTHIC, with a sworn duty to protect the world. And protect, she would! She'd tear threats limb from limb. Destroy them with her teeth and her best growl!

That's what she would do to Golden Jumpsuit, if they ever faced her again. They last saw her in the middle of the sea, so they probably would *never* see her again anyway. But if that evil fiend showed up—or if any other fiend showed up—Hailey would singlehandedly vanquish them. Mwahahaha!

Hailey looked back at her friends. Was it her

imagination, or had they not moved at all?! They were so slow up this mountain, they might as well be going BACKWARD.

How long was she supposed to wait? Her Mythie was expecting her.

Hailey bounced up on her toes. "I'm going to see what's ahead—"

"Don't you dare!" cried Ember from below. Hailey had known Ember for years. They went to the same elementary school in Cliffside Ledges. They had always been friendly but weren't friends until two weeks ago. First, because they were never in the same class. And second, because they hung out in different circles at recess. Ember spent her time playing kickball and delivering passionate speeches to the team when they were losing (and even when they were winning). Meanwhile, Hailey was part of the secret Daredevil Club that spent all their energy on daring competitions: who could swing the highest, who could jump the farthest, who could hang upside down on the monkey bars longest, and who could do the most flips underneath the slide.

The Daredevil Club got her in trouble, most especially when a

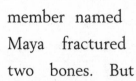

member named Maya fractured two bones. But hey—broken bones grow back even stronger. If anything, Maya's parents should have *thanked* her.

Anyway. It was kind of funny that Ember would

shout "don't you dare" to the self-appointed president, secretary, and treasurer of the Daredevil Club. Because . . . of course she dared!

She wasn't afraid of anything. Definitely not some craggy mountain. Hailey looked determinedly toward the top.

"Please, Hailey!" Pippa said, her voice loud but also gentle. Pippa was the sweetest person Hailey had ever met, and she would be a terrible member of the Daredevil Club. "We want to do things together. As a team."

"It's just . . . smarter if we all stick together!" Marina shouted. Marina was like Hailey's opposite person. Where Marina was cautious, Hailey was bold. Where Marina was quiet, Hailey was loud. Where Marina was anxious, Hailey was the surest, most assured person ever *in the world*.

But Hailey had to admit—Marina grew a lot during the quest for her kraken. When Hailey first met Marina, she had been afraid of her own shadow.

And now? Marina had a kraken monster on her back, and it didn't even faze her.

Hailey replied to Marina. "I want to get closer to my Mythie!"

"It's Ember's Mythie next, anyway!" Kit yelled. Hailey couldn't see Kit's eyes from this distance, but if she knew Kit at all—and she was sure she did—Kit was most definitely rolling them. Kit was sharp and witty and a little bit biting. Maybe not *daredevil* material, but she was all right in Hailey's book. "Ember's arrow is the brightest, Hailey. That's how this works!"

Arrow, schmarrow. Hailey wasn't going to let a little magic boss her around. Besides, the sooner they found Ember's familiar, the sooner they could get to Hailey's familiar. And if she could give everyone a head start, wasn't that better?

"Just meet me at the top!" Hailey shouted, and she ran ahead before any of her fellow Mythics could protest.

The climb got harder as the rocks became more

vertical and jagged. The air was starting to get dry and hot, but at least the view was nice. The mountains loomed tall to the north and west. To the east, there was the sea.

Hailey laughed. "This isn't so hard!" she said to nothing and no one. "And it definitely isn't scary."

She climbed and climbed and climbed. It felt good to be active. No, better than good—it felt *right*. Hailey had more energy and more enthusiasm than anyone she knew, and most times she didn't know where to put it.

The air was thick now and—almost smoky. Was it her imagination, or did it seem like the top of the mountain was moving? The clouds were wiggly. Were those clouds?

She quickened her pace. When she reached the top of the mountain, she noticed it was flat and hollow. There was a big hole in the center.

Hailey gasped. "It's not a mountain—it's a volcano!" she said to nothing and no one. She leaned over to get a closer look. Magma bubbled and burbled inside. Steam was rising, and the vapors were *hot*. Too hot.

Hailey coughed and scrambled to get away from the crater. Only, she lost her footing. She tried to get a grip or a foothold, but the entire rock crumbled away from the edge. And she was falling.

THE LEAST SURPRISING SURPRISE

"AHHHHHHHHH!" Hailey screamed as the magma got closer and closer and—

Something wrapped around her middle, and suddenly she was suspended in the air.

A kraken arm curled tightly around her.

And a giant, monstrous kraken stood on the lip of the volcano. Marina was missing, which meant that she had merged again with her familiar.

Kit, Pippa, and Ember were each holding on to the kraken tightly.

"We got you!" Ember cried, even though it looked

more like they were barely holding on.

"You are sooooo lucky familiar-travel is fast," Kit added. "We got here just in time!"

The kraken made a hissing noise and pulled Hailey up.

Then Marina, Kraken, and Hailey all collapsed outside the pit. They were panting.

"That was too scary!" Marina whimpered, pulling Kraken into a very squeezy hug. "We almost didn't make it, Hailey! What if we hadn't been fast enough?"

"But you *were* fast enough," Hailey said. She stood up and brushed herself off. "So, problem solved."

Every Mythic swiveled on her.

"Problem not solved!" Ember cried. "What were you thinking?!"

11

"We were worried about you," Pippa said.

"Seriously," Kit agreed. "You must have a death wish."

Marina frowned. "There's safety in numbers, Hailey. Without us, you would have been swimming in magma."

Hailey laughed. "But this is all part of a great adventure! The daring hero gets into a pickle and gets saved at the last possible moment. Sometimes you have to take risks."

Kit shook her head. "But not *all* the time."

Of course, *all* the time. Life was one giant risk, and every choice led to one giant payoff. That was what it meant to be daring and bold! Besides, how could Kit, Ember, Marina, and Pippa even expect to find the rest of the Mythies and save the world without taking a risk?

Or . . . was this about something else? This moment felt familiar, and—with a twinge—Hailey remembered that sometimes the places that were supposed to be her havens . . . weren't. Sometimes she felt so different. Even within the Daredevil Club, even within her own house.

At school, the Daredevil Club gave her energy and purpose—but often her dares were vetoed by the other members of the club for being *too much*.

At home, she felt like the odd one out. Her mom and stepdad never compared her to her sisters, but there was a difference. Hailey knew. Her older sister, Nova, was a calm, measured person. Her younger sister, Willow, was a snuggly, cuddly person.

And now, with the Mythics, it was that same feeling again. Even when she was among her people, sometimes she felt alo—

Hailey shook her head.

No. She wasn't going to think about that.

Hailey didn't have to be like her sisters, and she didn't have to be like her friends. She worked differently. That was okay. She knew who she was.

She jutted her chin and looked up defiantly, but

no one was concerned with her anymore. Everyone was gazing into the volcano. Hailey crawled over to peer at, well, what everyone else was peering at.

"So," Kit said wryly, "I think it's safe to say this is Lavaside Rocks."

"What in the world could my Mythie be?" Ember wondered, looking at her arrow. It was still pointing straight ahead, blazing brighter than ever, almost like Ember was holding sunshine.

Marina began to shiver nervously. "Does this look . . . active to you?" she asked with a gulp.

Come to think of it, the magma inside the volcano did seem a bit too gurgly. It reminded Hailey of whenever her mom heated tomato sauce on the stove: bubbles and then . . .

"It's gonna blow!" Hailey cried.

BOOM.

The volcano erupted in a plume of black smoke. They all cowered. Hailey and Pippa began coughing uncontrollably. Kit hid her nose inside her shirt.

Marina tried to protect them by making a wall of water. It guarded them for a moment, but then, in the heat of the eruption, the shield began to bubble and evaporate.

The temperature was sweltering. As the lava dripped down the other side of the volcano, Hailey wiped the sweat from her brow. If only she had the power to *help* in some way. Instead of standing here like a useless piece of string cheese. She wanted to be like Marina, who was doing an *awesome* job saving her friends. Except, unlike Marina, Hailey wouldn't whimper while fighting the elements.

Only Ember seemed undeterred as the volcano sputtered. She stood tall. Maybe she felt her Mythie's presence nearby and knew she was protected.

Hailey was awed. And envious. And proud.

"GO, EMBER!" she shouted.

Ember held up her palm. Her arrow was spinning quickly. Hailey tried to follow it with her eyes, but it made her dizzy.

Then Ember's hand erupted with dazzling, blinding light.

"OUCH!" she shrieked, pulling her right hand into her body and cradling it with her left arm.

Marina sucked in a sharp breath. "This is it—exactly what happened when Kraken was nearby!"

"Check the lava!" Hailey cried, and they all crawled to the lip of the volcano, scanning the lava for any signs of movement.

"What are we looking for?" Kit asked.

"I dunno!" Hailey said. "A magma monster? A lava snake? Ooo—a lava lamp!"

Kit snorted. "A lava lamp?"

"That would be SO COOL!"

"I can't see anything," Pippa said, wiping her steaming glasses. "Ember?"

Ember wasn't staring down. She was staring up.

The smoke above began to take the shape of a giant bird.

Hailey grinned. "Wicked!"

"It's too high up! I can't reach it! It's not like I can fly—how do I get it?"

"You don't," said a voice.

They whipped around. It was the least surprising surprise. Right behind them, properly on cue, there she was:

Golden Jumpsuit.

WHAT GOES UP . . .

Hailey's first thought was that Golden Jumpsuit had seen better days. Her long hair was tied back in a crusty-looking ponytail. Her eyes were sunken, and she had some scrapes on her cheek. Her scowl was intense. The only thing about Golden Jumpsuit that didn't seem sea-tousled was her outfit. Golden Jumpsuit's golden jumpsuit was, again, flawless. It glimmered and danced in the light of the lava.

Hailey's second thought was a loud one. "GET AWAY FROM MY FRIENDS!" she shouted, jumping in front of Pippa and Marina.

Golden Jumpsuit looked her up and down. Hailey *hated* that look. It was the look of someone underestimating her.

"You don't even have a Mythie," Golden Jumpsuit snorted. "You have no beast and no powers. What can *you* do?"

"THIS!" Hailey said, and she ran forward and tackled Golden Jumpsuit around the middle.

They tumbled backward, toward the crater of the volcano. Marina, Pippa, and Kit cried out.

"HAILEY!"

Golden Jumpsuit looked at her with surprise. And then triumph.

Which was confusing because Hailey knew she was winning.

She was braver and stronger than *anyone*, especially the likes of foul Golden Jumpsuit.

"Give up, you fiend! I've got you cornered—" Hailey cut off. She was suddenly more tired than she'd ever felt in her whole life. Her limbs were like spaghetti. She flopped off Golden Jumpsuit, and try as she might, she couldn't get her body to *move*.

She couldn't even speak. Her tongue was tired . . . something she'd never experienced before IN HER LIFE.

Golden Jumpsuit stood up, brushed herself off, and grabbed Hailey by the ankle.

Inside her head, Hailey was kicking and scream-ing. But outside her head, she hung upside down like a wet noodle.

"You alone would never defeat me," Golden Jumpsuit said coldly, carrying Hailey toward the hollow of the volcano. "Goodbye."

A stream of water came gushing her way from a gigantic kraken. The water hit Golden Jumpsuit in the face, and she dropped Hailey.

Hailey lay on the ground as Kit and Pippa ran to her. They each grabbed an armpit and dragged Hailey away from the gurgling magma.

"Wait!" Hailey groaned. "I can still—fight her."

"Hailey, you can barely stand!" Kit said, but Hailey pretended not to hear.

"Let me—at her—"

Pippa gave Hailey's arm a gentle squeeze as she continued to pull her away from the villain.

Golden Jumpsuit pressed a button on her boots, and they began to roar. And just like that, she took flight—toward the smoke in the shape of a bird.

"My Mythie!" Ember cried, throwing her arms up to the sky. She was beckoning her Mythie to come home to her, but the smoke outline of the bird did not move, and the villain was getting farther away, and the magma was rising higher.

"Think," Marina whispered.

"No, move!" Hailey cried as the mountain spit up a dribble of lava that was coming right toward them.

They dodged to the side, just in time! A stream of lava came flowing down, right where they had been standing.

The volcano was scorchingly, blisteringly hot. There weren't even words, Hailey thought, for how hot it was. Maybe "boilroastingfiresizzle." Everyone

except Ember was dripping sweat, and Hailey started panting. Hey, if it worked for dogs . . . she might as well try it.

Kit groaned. "Is this what bacon feels like?"

Ember turned around. "Marina, how do I get up there? How do I beat Golden Jumpsuit to my Mythie?"

Marina held her head, her face all scrunched up. "I . . . I don't know!"

"There has to be a way," Pippa said.

"It's impossible," Kit said. "It's not like we have a jetpack or a familiar that could fly us there . . ."

Hailey thought hard. They didn't have jetpack boots like Golden Jumpsuit, but they had something Golden Jumpsuit did not. A monster with brute strength.

She started laughing madly—almost a full-blown cackle. "I have an idea," Hailey said. "A really fun one!"

Kit looked at her with a sideways glance. "Is it dangerous?"

"Of course!" Hailey said.

"I don't care—it's the only option we've got!" Ember said, watching as Golden Jumpsuit disappeared into the smoke. The bird above them made a squawking cry. "Hurry!"

"We need the Mythical Monster of Monstrosity!" Hailey said. When everyone looked at her with confusion, she clarified. "Marina and Kraken melded together."

"Oh, right!" Marina said as she and Kraken bonded in a burst of light. Marina disappeared, and the kraken was massive.

"Okay," Hailey said, wrapping one of Kraken's arms around Ember. "Now, I'm going to need you to throw Ember."

"What?!" Kit said.

Pippa grabbed Ember's hand. "There has to be a better way."

Even Marina let out a bubble in protest.

"NO TIME!" Hailey said as the bird cawed in

distress. "Wind up . . . and pitch!"

Ember nodded. Marina sling-shot Ember up into the sky. Up, up, up—Ember went so high that she disappeared into the smoke.

It was all so exciting that Hailey could barely stand it. She whooped and hollered toward the sky. What an adventure!

And then—"AHHHHHHHHHHHH!"

A piercing scream rang through the sky as something shot out of the smoke. It was Ember. What went up was finally coming down.

THE BIRD

"We have to do something!" Kit cried. "Ember's plummeting!"

"Okay, Marina," Hailey said, turning to the giant kraken. "Here's the plan. Throw me, and I'll catch Ember in the air."

"But who's going to catch you?" Kit asked.

"Hmmm . . . good point. Okay. Throw me to catch Ember. Throw Pippa to catch me. Throw Kit to catch Pippa. And then throw yourself to catch Kit. Boom—solved it!"

"You're creating more problems!" Kit yelled.

"But we love your creativity," Pippa added.

"Blub," Marina said. She pointed one of her eight arms at Ember, who was dropping like an asteroid.

"NO!" Golden Jumpsuit cried. Her voice echoed like thunder, and the sky erupted in a flash of orange flames. Ember was suspended in midair as a long rope of fire wrapped itself around her ankle.

"Awesome!" Hailey said.

Ember touched her hand to the fire. And a light blazed so bright that Hailey had to look away. This was just like when Marina bonded with the kraken.

A huge gust of wind followed the light, blowing all the smoke away. And then, hovering above the volcano, was an enormous bird on fire.

"A phoenix!" Marina gasped.

Marina had unbonded with the kraken, and Hailey hadn't even noticed. No offense to Marina and her kraken, but there was a shiny *new* Mythie in town. And Hailey couldn't take her eyes off it.

"A phoenix?" Pippa asked.

"It's a fiery sun bird that's supposed to be immortal. When it dies, it's reborn from the ashes."

Hailey squealed, "I. WANT. IT." How could this not be her Mythie? It was *perfect*.

The Ember-phoenix let out a squawk. She swooped toward Golden Jumpsuit, who was trying to lasso the bird with a rope.

"GO, EMBER!" Hailey shouted.

"You can do it!" Pippa cheered.

"Watch out for the rope!" Marina warned. "And the jetpacks! And the lava! Just . . . watch out!"

"And don't look down!" Kit added. "What?" She shrugged when everyone looked at her. "I feel about heights the same way I feel about boats—no thank you."

Golden Jumpsuit threw the rope around Ember's talon. There was a collective gasp from the Mythics on the ground, but there was nothing anyone could do about it. Ember was too high up, and no one else was airborne.

Golden Jumpsuit let out a triumphant, "Ha! Got you!"

She yanked the rope. Ember was jerked to the left. But then! Ember let out a breath, and a jet of fire burned the rope to dust. With a flap of her wing, Ember knocked one of the jetpack boots off

Golden Jumpsuit's foot. The sudden imbalance sent Golden Jumpsuit spinning out of the sky and away from the mountain.

"HOORAY!" Hailey yelled. "Villainy is foiled once again!"

Ember landed on the edge of the volcano, in front of them. She raised her wings. Instantly, the eruption calmed. The magma stopped spluttering, and the lava stopped flowing. It hardened into black rock.

"Squawk! Caw! Caw!" Ember the phoenix said.

Kit and Pippa looked alarmed. Marina looked like she understood Ember. Hailey squealed with excitement for her friend. "Ember, you LEGEND!"

At last, Ember and her Mythie unbonded, and Ember lay flat on the volcanic rock, gasping for air. "That was terrifying."

The phoenix—so tiny and cute—flew to Ember and perched on her finger.

"Ashley, meet everyone. Everyone, meet Ashley."

"Ashley?" Kit asked.

"It's her name."

Everyone turned to Marina. "Wait," Kit said. "Does your kraken have a name? Because I've been calling her Kraken for like two weeks now."

"It's Kraken," Marina said. "Her name is Kraken."

Pshhhh. Her friends may have awesome Mythies of awesomeness, but they were *terrible* at naming their companions. Hailey would show them. Just as soon as she got her . . .

She put her hand out. Pippa and Kit did the same. Hailey's hand was more dazzling than a star. Much brighter than all the other arrows.

"My turn! My turn!" She ran forward. She had to follow her arrow! She knew only one mode: go, go, GOOOOOOO.

"Augh!" She tripped over a rock, rolled ten feet down the volcano, and skinned her knee.

"Hailey, are you okay?" Pippa cried as they all started carefully descending the volcano.

Hailey checked herself out. Her knee was bleeding. That could be fixed—good thing Mom always made her keep first aid stuff in her vest pocket.

She spit on the wound to clean it, then she put two bandages over it in an X. There. Good as new.

Nothing was going to stop her. Not Golden Jumpsuit, not a volcano, not even . . .

"Ow." She winced as she stood to her feet. Her ankle felt funny. And not the good kind of funny.

"Hailey, I'm so glad you're all right," Pippa said as the other Mythics finally caught up with her. She helped brush the dirt and ash off Hailey.

Pippa is, Hailey thought, *a very good person.*

"Thwarted by the evil volcano!" Hailey grumbled.

Ember and Kit exchanged a look. The same look that Hailey's mom often gave her stepdad. The same look that her big sis often gave her little sis.

"Um, Hailey?" Marina said in a tiny voice. "You kind of . . . you've been . . ."

"You're thwarting yourself!" Kit interrupted.

Hailey shifted uncomfortably. "I'm fine." She laughed nice and loud, just to prove it. "All good."

Ember put a hand on Hailey's back, and Ashley the phoenix let out a somber cry. "Look, Hailey, you're part of a team now, and you don't have to do this all alone."

"We're concerned, that's all," Pippa said.

Ember nodded. "You're going to get seriously hurt if you keep jumping into the fray like that. You can't do the daredevil thing anymore."

"But I'm not afraid of anything."

"But *we* are," Marina said. Because of course Marina said that—she was afraid of everything.

Hailey looked around at her friends. Marina winced. Pippa avoided her gaze. Ember frowned deeply. Kit stared at her. In fact, her eyes darted to Hailey's skinned knee, down to her twisted ankle, and back up again to her face. She looked very much like she had something on her mind.

At last she crossed her arms and said, "Hailey, you dive into danger. You act without thinking."

Hailey snorted. "Name one time!"

"The time you nearly fell into lava before Marina saved you."

"Okay, but you can't name two times!" Hailey said.

Kit sighed. "The time you charged at Golden

Jumpsuit, and she basically caused you to collapse. The time you launched Ember into the sky without a plan. The time you tumbled down the mountain and clearly twisted your ankle."

"Whaaaaat?" Hailey said. "My ankle is fine—no, it's great—no, it's perfect—no, it's THE HEALTH-IEST, UNINJUREDEST ANKLE THAT HAS EVER EXISTED."

"We just don't want you to get hurt," Pippa said.

Kit, Marina, and Ember murmured in agreement.

Hailey knew she could shrug off a skinned knee and laugh away a twisted ankle, but she felt hurt on the *inside*, and that was so much harder to ignore.

It sounded like they all wanted her to change. *But,* she thought, as stubborn defiance flushed within her, *I'm not going to.*

This was why she always did things all by herself. That way, she could never feel the disappointment when she wasn't the person others expected her to be—or wanted her to be. She knew who she was, and she felt good about it too.

She was used to being different from everyone else. The only person in her family like her. The only person at school like her. And even in this group of girls who were in the *exact same* boat as her, Hailey still stuck out like a crooked nail. Just like always.

She could depend on herself, though, she thought as she tested her wobbly ankle. Fearless and daring heroes were rarely understood, and they always came out strong in the end. She would find her Mythie, help the Mythics, and save the world—even if she had to do it alone.

5

ESCAPE

As Hailey stretched out her ankle, Ashley the phoenix let out an urgent cry from Ember's shoulder.

"We have to go. Now," Marina whispered, straining to look across the volcano.

She didn't have to say it. They were all thinking it. *Golden Jumpsuit.*

"Come on, Hailey," Ember said. "Let's go get your Mythie."

Hailey examined her arrow. It was pointing west—toward the setting sun. What was west again?

Splashside Falls, Mountainside Snows, Tundraside Frosts. What sort of Mythie could be living in the cold over there?

No time to think about it. Ember and Ashley melded together and became superphoenix. They wrapped their left claw around Hailey and Kit and their right claw around Pippa and Marina. Kraken braided her arms into Marina's hair, tugging tightly. And then they were off!

They rose higher and higher. Above the volcanoes, below the clouds, where the air was thin and crisp. The Mythics soared through the sky, leaving a streak of flames behind them like a crimson rainbow.

"Ember? Your butt is on fire," Hailey said, then she burst into a cackling laugh.

"Oh no," Marina groaned. "Can you turn off your tail flames, Ember? This is like leaving Golden Jumpsuit a path straight to us."

"Caw!" Ember said, wiggling her tail feathers

until the fire went out, and the streaks behind them disappeared. But Ember's wings were still alight. It was impossible to dull a fire beast.

The sky was a lot colder than Hailey thought it would be, but it was *exhilarating*. Maybe the best adventure she'd taken in her whole life, and that included the SS *Seashanty*. Hailey whooped and hollered and relished the wind. But being trapped in Ember's left claw with Kit meant she kept hearing "Don't look down, don't look down. Oh no—*why* did I look down?"

"Don't worry, you won't fall," Hailey said.

Kit gulped. "Really?"

"Sure. Ember's got you. And if she doesn't, you'll have the first, last, and best skydive of your life all at the same time."

Kit moaned and closed her eyes.

They flew for a long time. The volcanoes became tiny summits behind them. Below, the flat mountains were both mossy and rocky. Water flowed off the top and pooled at the bottom. Some of the waterfalls were nothing more than dribbles. Some were violent bursts. Everywhere Hailey looked, it was waterfall after waterfall. Hundreds of them, it seemed like.

She wondered what it would be like to jump off a waterfall—to plunge straight down into the lake below.

And then, in front of them—nestled in a valley between five waterfalls—was a town.

"Is this the town center of Splashside Falls?" Pippa asked curiously.

"It has to be!" Hailey said as Ember began to descend. Hailey tugged on Ember's talon. "Hey, why are we stopping?"

Every eye looked at her. Even the phoenix stared her down.

"Seriously?" Kit said. "We need food."

"And rest," Pippa added.

"And shelter," Marina said, nervously scouting the land below them.

"And Ember must be tired," Pippa said. "Now that we've put some distance between us and Golden Jumpsuit, we should give Ember a break. She's been doing a lot of hard work today."

Ember let out a grateful "Caw!"

Hailey harrumphed. *Fine*, but they had better be on the move first thing tomorrow morning.

They landed on the outskirts of Splashside Falls and ventured into town. It reminded Hailey a bit of Seaside Sands. Both towns were on the smaller side—way smaller than her hometown of Cliffside Ledges. Both Splashside Falls and Seaside Sands were packed with rows and rows of stone cottages. And both were right beside the water.

In fact, this whole town seemed to be covered in a misty spray; it looked almost magical. But the noise

Hailey could live without. Five waterfalls were very loud. Hailey felt like she needed to shout to be heard.

"NOW WHAT?" she asked.

"Food?" Kit suggested.

Ember and Marina exchanged a look. Then Ember unzipped her fanny pack, while Marina removed the sole of her shoe. They both counted the only money that didn't sink with the rest of their supplies when the SS *Seashanty* went down.

Marina frowned. "We don't have *that* much left."

Kit's stomach growled. "Do we have enough for a meal, though? That's the only thing I care about."

"We have enough for a lot of meals," Marina said. "But we shouldn't buy any. We should eat one of our tins of fish."

"Sardines?!" Kit groaned. "Again?"

Hailey made a puking noise, and Pippa smiled weakly.

"We have to budget for the rest of our adventure . . . which might be weeks. Or months. Or years. What if we run out of money too soon? What'll we do if we have a *real* emergency? What if we need to purchase something to stop Golden Jumpsuit? What if we need to buy shelter, supplies, or food later?"

Ugh, Marina was so responsible. *Too* responsible.

"But there won't *be* a later on if we starve today!" Kit said. "And don't you dare mention those sardine tins again—"

"Kit, they're here and they're free . . ."

Hailey watched them quarrel, but she stopped

listening. Her wheels were turning. If only there was a way they could get stuff without spending any money. Like, maybe if they saved someone's life, they'd be so grateful that *of course* they'd feed their rescuers . . .

Except. Wasn't that exactly what they were already doing? I mean, they hadn't saved anyone *yet*, but they would. Soon. They were the intrepid heroes of Terrafamiliar! Someone ought to throw them a bone! (Hopefully one with meat on it.)

"Leave it to me!" Hailey said, interrupting Marina and Kit's dispute. "I have an idea!"

THE FANS

"What idea?" Kit said skeptically.

"That's for me to know and you to find out. Now, come on!" Hailey tried to strut, but her ankle was still feeling funky, so it was more like a limp. The other Mythics followed her. *Good*, Hailey thought. She could prove them wrong—and show them how awesomely awesome of a leader she could be.

She marched inside the nearest café. There were rows of sandwiches behind the display case, and Hailey's mouth watered. When she reached the front of the line, she put her elbows on the counter and smiled brightly at the man working the register, his beaver familiar gnawing gashes in the countertop.

"Hi, hello, good sir!" Hailey said. "I can see you are very busy, and I will only take a moment of your time. We five"—she gestured behind her—"are valiant heroes, destined to save the world. Which includes you. And this café. And all the citizens of all the towns in Terrafamiliar. As such, we will be requiring five free sandwiches."

"I can't just give you free sandwiches." His gaze traveled to Ember. Then he stared at Marina. "What kind of familiars are those?"

"That's Ashley the phoenix and Kraken the kraken."

"Phoenix? Kraken? Are those real?"

"They're real for us."

"And who are you?"

Hailey leaned in. She lowered her voice. "I'll let you in on a little secret. We're the Mythics!"

The man snorted. "No, you're not. Stop trying to scam me for free food." Then he went into the back of the store.

Hailey turned around. Her face was flush. This was *supposed* to work. "I thought being a hero would have more . . . glory, fame, and fortune!" Hailey admitted. "And a lot less tinned fish! We're *the Mythics*— you'd think that'd be worth five sandwiches!"

"Wait, you're Mythics?" said a young woman from the next table over. She quickly turned around to get a good look at them. She seemed to be just past her teen years, with pinkish skin and messy brown hair. She was a burly, muscular sort of person, which seemed to match the impressively massive grizzly bear familiar curled up by her feet. "Truly?"

Pippa nodded.

"Indeed we are, honorable civilian!" Hailey said grandly.

The woman elbowed her friend excitedly. "Darius—they're the *Mythics*!"

"You've heard of us?" Ember said, surprised.

"Who hasn't?" she said. She jumped to her feet. "Word of the five girls who didn't get familiars this year traveled faster than the speed of sound! But the last we heard, the Mythics headed straight into the ocean. We hoped we'd meet you one day, but we never thought you'd come to *our* town. My name is Bernadette, by the way."

"I'm Darius," said the young man. He stood up in a very graceful motion. He had dark tan skin and

striking eyes that matched the color of the scales on his green anaconda familiar.

"Whoa!" said Hailey, noticing the snake under the table. She'd never seen a serpent this long or this thick before. It seemed twenty feet long, or maybe even longer. Too bad it wasn't a mythical beast, because it was extremely cool. In a monstrous sort of way.

Bernadette gave Darius a hopeful look. Then she addressed the Mythics. "Did we overhear you correctly? You're looking for a meal? Darius and I are roommates. We live right around the corner—we can give you food and a place to stay for the night. If it's okay with you, Darius?"

"Absolutely," Darius said quickly. "It would be our honor. We have an extra bed, two couches, and a recliner chair."

"Please," Bernadette said. "We're just such big fans. We want to help you in any way we can. Please let us do this for you. What do you say?"

"Oh, no," Marina said. "Thanks anyway."

"That would be wonderful!" Pippa said at the same time.

Marina and Pippa looked at each other. Stalemate.

"Would you excuse us for a minute?" Ember said, and the five Mythics huddled in the corner of the café to talk as the man at the register emerged with a broom and began to sweep up. His beaver was helping, using his tail to scoot the dust. Clearly, the store was going to close soon.

"I think we should go to their house," Ember whispered. "We don't know anyone in Splashside Falls, and we have no shelter, and I don't know about you, but I'm already tired of sleeping on the ground outside."

"Remember the warning Mayor

Mejor gave me? About not trusting anyone but each other? About how we're in grave danger?" Marina squeaked. "Well, stranger danger!"

"But Mayor Loch told me to keep my heart open," Pippa said. "I think we should trust the people we're trying to save. They did say they were fans, and they seem helpful and kind."

"If we're voting, I'm with Marina!" Hailey said quickly. "I don't want to stay here for *any* amount of time. I want to go straight to my Mythie! In fact, we should leave! Right now! Hurry up! Faster!"

Everyone looked at Kit, the tie-breaking vote. She winced. "I'm for any plan that gets us food. Sorry, Marina. Sorry, Hailey."

Hailey pouted.

"Then it's settled," Ember said. She turned to Bernadette and Darius, who were across the café pretending like they weren't listening even when they obviously were. "We're coming!"

Bernadette and Darius weren't lying when they

said their house was around the corner. Just as Ember had finished thanking their hosts, they arrived at the cottage doorstep.

Their house was small, messy, and dark. Darius scurried about, turning on lights and tidying up. "I'm sorry," he said. "We weren't expecting visitors, or I would have cleaned."

"Girls, I'll boil some noodles for you," Bernadette said. "Make yourselves at home on the couch. And here—I have some clams for your kraken and seeds for your phoenix. I'll put them in the corner."

Kraken and Ashley hopped over to the corner and began to eat.

Hailey sat in between Ember and Pippa. It was a tight squeeze, all of them on one couch, but the sofa was a large one. It wasn't like they had another option, anyway; the lounge chair was covered with a laundry pile.

Watching Darius flit around the room was making Hailey dizzy. He was picking up all sorts of dirty clothes and cleaning some plates, and his familiar

was following him around as he circled the couch.
Then the snake got overexcited and jumped up onto
their legs.

Hailey yelped as its smooth, muscly body slith-
ered across her lap.

"Um . . . ," Marina said. Panic was rising in her
voice. But Hailey didn't think snakes were *that* gross.

"Do you all like red sauce with your noodles,"
Bernadette called from the kitchen, "or do you want
butter?"

"Red sauce is great," Ember said politely. "Thank
you so much."

"Um . . . ," Marina said again. "Everyone?"

The green anaconda was curling around the couch. Kind of like . . . a seat belt. There was a sudden squeeze as the serpent coiled a little tighter around them.

"Darius?" Kit said. "Can you come get your snake?"

"What's that?" he called from the kitchen.

"I said, *come get your familiar before it strangles us to death*!"

Darius and Bernadette appeared in the doorway.

"But," Darius said with a creepy grin, "that's exactly the idea!"

A SNAKE IN THE GRASS

"I don't understand," Pippa said. "You were just pretending to be our friends?"

"It's nothing personal," Bernadette said. "We just have a job to do."

The green anaconda contracted. He crushed Hailey so tight, she thought she was seeing fireflies. "Unhand us—you fiends—" she gasped.

"Kraken!" Marina called to her familiar, but Bernadette snapped her fingers, and the grizzly bear moved. With its sharp claws, it grabbed Kraken's bulbous head in one paw—and Ashley by the throat in the other.

"Ashley!" Ember cried.

Both Ashley and Kraken were tiny—unable to reach their Mythics to morph into their beast forms. The phoenix made a mournful sound, and the kraken burbled. The grizzly did not let go.

Kit shook her head confusedly. "What are you—why are you—?"

"Shhhhhhh, save your breath," Darius said. "My familiar here can crush your little lungs in an instant. Of course, he's restraining . . . for now." He turned to Bernadette. "Did you contact the Boss?"

"Of course I did. I'm sure she's on her way."

The Boss? Who was *the Boss*? And why did Hailey have this awful, squirmy feeling that it was exactly who she thought it was?

"We have to go!" Hailey choked out. Ember and Marina looked at her hopelessly, and Kit and Pippa looked at her helplessly. Hailey would just have to show them how it's done.

She leaned forward and bit the snake as hard as she could.

The anaconda hissed angrily, and Hailey wriggled with all her might. It was still too strong for her, but her action broke Ember and Marina out of their fear.

Marina summoned a water bubble between her stomach and the snake's body—just just big enough to create a pocket of space, so she could crawl out. Ember let out a long fiery breath and scorched the snake's back. It flailed and loosened its grip.

59

Darius shrieked in rage. He cradled his snake.

But Hailey didn't have time to watch him. She had to save her friends' Mythies from a grisly grizzly. Hailey made her way toward the bear. It roared in her face, leaving spittle all over her.

"Gross!" Hailey said. "But you can't fight me and hold on to those Mythies at the same time!" And she punched the bear in the stomach.

The bear let go of Ashley and Kraken. It snarled angrily at Hailey as she backed away quickly.

Whoops! She hadn't thought this out. Could she outrun a bear?

Then the bear barreled toward her.

With her hand, Ember shoved Hailey out of the way—just in time. And with her left arm, she made a flinging motion. A fireball appeared and soared toward the grizzly—but it narrowly missed. It hit the wall instead. And the house started to catch fire.

"Oops!" Ember said. "I can't aim that well with my left!"

"EVERYONE OUT!" Kit yelled.

It was chaos—everyone pushing everyone else aside, trying to escape the burning cottage. They tumbled outside—the Mythics, the Mythies, the bear, the snake, and the not-actually-fans.

Quickly, the small cottage was ablaze.

"Sorry!" Pippa said to Bernadette and Darius.

"Pippa, they *betrayed us*!" Hailey shouted.

"I know, but I still feel sorry for burning their house down!"

"At least we got out in time," Ember said.

But Hailey quickly realized they were out of the fire and into a bigger one. Because when they turned

around, standing before them—hands on her hips—
was a familiar figure.

"Boss!" Darius said, bowing his head.

Yes, there she was. Shimmering in the evening
lamplight. Yet again.

Golden Jumpsuit.

Kit stomped her foot. "Stop. Following. Us."

Golden Jumpsuit ignored Kit. Instead, she
looked at Bernadette, who withered under Golden

Jumpsuit's golden-eyed gaze. "You couldn't keep them contained?"

"They're too skilled."

"They're *children*. Three of them don't even have familiars."

"Sorry, Boss." Bernadette lowered her chin.

"Did you call the other sympathizers in Splashside Falls?"

"Er, no, Boss—we didn't think we'd need anyone else's help."

"Sorry," Darius squeaked.

Golden Jumpsuit scowled. "When you want something done right . . ." She ran toward Marina. "I'll take care of it myself!"

Marina squeaked. She tried to bond with Kraken, but Golden Jumpsuit grabbed her by the wrist.

"Unhand her!" Hailey yelled, trying to pull Marina out of Golden Jumpsuit's grip. But there was no need. In fear, in panic, Kraken released one massive ink squirt—right into Golden Jumpsuit's eyes.

Golden Jumpsuit let go, and Kraken spurted more ink. The messy black liquid covered Golden Jumpsuit head to toe—from her scrunchie to the tips of her boots.

Golden Jumpsuit screamed furiously.

Free from Golden Jumpsuit's grip, Marina let water pour from her hands, a constant stream of it. "Ember!"

On cue, Ember heated up the water. Splashside Falls—an already misty place—filled with dense, thick, hot fog. Hailey could barely see the tip of her nose, let alone anyone else.

It was just like Kraken's ink cloud, only this smoke screen covered a much larger area. It was exactly what they needed to escape.

The five Mythics linked arms and ran through the haze.

UNDER THE FALLS

They didn't stop running. Not for a long while. Not until they had passed four different waterfalls. Hailey's ankle was throbbing.

"Do you think we lost her?" Pippa panted.

"Please," Kit said. "You think we escaped her *that* easily?"

"Well?" Ember said, looking to Marina. She always looked to Marina for plans, Hailey thought grumpily. But Marina wasn't the one who *bit* a snake tonight. That might be the most dangerously daring thing Hailey had ever done.

Marina looked around. She twisted her hair nervously. "Um . . . I don't think we can fly. She'll see us. You light up the sky with your flames, Ember. And I don't think we can run anymore. We're all so tired and sluggish. And besides, Hailey's ankle—"

"My ankle is better than it has *ever* been before in my whole life!" Hailey lied.

"Uh-huh," Kit said skeptically.

Marina squinted toward one of the six waterfalls up ahead. She and Kraken merged together, and Marina slunk into the pool of water at the bottom of the falls. She disappeared, and when she emerged again, she beckoned the Mythics to hop on.

But Hailey didn't need Marina's help. She never asked for help, if she could help it. She was perfectly capable of doing everything on her own, thank you very much.

Hailey dove into the chilly water. She kicked and paddled to the waterfall, which plummeted hard on her head. She took a deep breath and dove. She swam, swam, swam—pushing her way under the falls until she popped out on the other side. There was a hollow. A tiny cave. This must be what Marina and Kraken had found.

She turned around as a giant kraken entered the cave under the waterfall, carrying Kit, Pippa, and Ember (shielding Ashley from the water as much as possible).

"If Golden Jumpsuit followed us across the ocean and up a volcano, don't you think she'll look behind waterfalls for us?" Kit asked. "You really think we're safe here?"

Marina squirmed. "Well, there are so many waterfalls to check, and we can take turns keeping lookout? And . . . I don't think we're safe *anywhere*."

She groaned. Then under her breath, Marina started rattling off all the things that could go wrong. Hailey thought she heard something about vampire bats, drowning after sleepwalking into the waterfalls, and flesh-eating bacteria . . . but it was hard to hear over the sound of the rushing water.

"We're okay," Ember said. She put a reassuring hand on Marina's shoulder. Then she moved deeper into the cave and started a fire in her palm. "Come— let's dry off and eat."

Except . . . they had nothing to eat but Marina's two tins of sardines from the SS *Seashanty*. They were back to square one! They were quiet as they opened a tin and passed it around.

Hailey took a fish. She cringed as she dangled it in front of her face. If she never

saw a sardine again it would be *too soon*.

"So," Marina said, slurping down a slimy sardine, "are we going to talk about how bad this is?"

"I was just thinking that!" Hailey said excitedly. "I never *ever* want to eat fish again."

Marina shook her head. "Not that! The fact that Golden Jumpsuit has followers!"

"Oh."

"Technically, she said 'sympathizers,'" Kit pointed out.

"Sympathizers, followers, minions, cronies, sub-ordinates, underlings, henchpeople—it's all the same thing!" Marina said, her voice rising in panic. She was shaking. Kraken burrowed under Marina's shirt. The Mythie was feeding off Marina's energy. "It means Golden Jumpsuit has spies! We can't trust anyone but each other! We're all alone!"

"Nothing's changed. We were always alone," Ember said. "Isn't that what Mayor Mejor said to you? That there were people out there who would want to take our power?"

"Yes, but . . . ," Pippa said thoughtfully. She took a moment to formulate her idea. "When we said goodbye, my mayor—Mayor Loch—told me not to lose faith in people. That there will always be people around who will help us."

Hailey wasn't sure she had ever exchanged more than two words with her mayor, let alone heeded his advice. Hailey looked between Marina and Pippa. "You both have weird friendships with your mayors."

Marina shrugged.

"Mayor Loch also runs the library," Pippa said, "so I used to run into her a lot."

"Your mayor has a second job as a librarian?" Hailey laughed.

"She was a librarian before she got elected, but then she didn't want to give it up—"

"Back to the *point*," Kit interrupted. "Which is that anyone could be a spy for Golden Jumpsuit."

"And more terrifying," Ember added, "is that Golden Jumpsuit already has so much more power than we even realized."

They grew quiet. The only sounds were the crackling fire and the hushing waterfall.

"Well," Ember continued, as if she was deciding something. "We will just have to keep a lower profile. And maybe we shouldn't announce to the world that we're Mythics."

Everyone looked at Hailey.

"ME?!" Hailey said. This was an unfair sneak attack. "You can't blame me! That wasn't my fault!"

Ember inched closer to the fire to rekindle it. Ashley chirped on her shoulder. "I'm just saying maybe we don't have to share our situation . . . quite so loudly. Or even at all. Then we wouldn't have to worry about the wrong people overhearing."

Hailey harrumphed. "I didn't want to go back to Darius and Bernadette's creepy little house in the first place! Marina and I voted to leave, remember?"

Kit and Ember looked at her like they weren't convinced, and Pippa's eyes were shining with sympathy. Marina looked down at her shoes.

A hard lump formed in Hailey's throat. Suddenly, her brain swam with a memory—the time the Daredevil Club told her that her dares were too much. *She* was too much. This was just like that moment.

And suddenly, she didn't want to be here anymore.

"I'm going to bed," Hailey announced.

"Great idea," Ember said, sounding relieved that the awkwardness had broken.

They curled up by the fire, while Marina took first watch. But Hailey couldn't sleep. She couldn't explain it. At first, she felt really hot and embarrassed by the whole day. And then that feeling blew away. And then she felt sad and disappointed. But that feeling blew away too.

And then she couldn't help but think about *real* problems, like Golden Jumpsuit.

She got up and tiptoed to the pool of water behind the falls, where Marina was keeping watch with Kraken.

"Hailey, is that you?"

"Shhhhh!" Hailey hissed. She didn't want to wake the others.

Marina sighed in relief. "You scared me!" She swirled her toes in the water, and it looked kind of fun, so Hailey took off her shoes and stuck her feet in too. The water felt so good on her swollen, twisted ankle.

Kraken crawled from Marina's shoulder to Hailey's.

"Hi, little buddy!" Hailey said, softly petting Kraken on the head. Kraken let out a bubble of delight.

"Couldn't sleep?" Marina asked.

"Nope. There's too much to do. Too much to plan."

Marina smiled at her knowingly. "You're also thinking about Golden Jumpsuit."

Hailey shook her head. "I'm done with thinking—I'm ready to do something about her."

A silence fell between them. Well, as silent as it could possibly be under a waterfall.

"Maybe we can do something," Marina said finally. "You fought her."

"So did you."

"But not long enough. It was just a second. So, what was it like, Hailey?"

"I dunno," Hailey said with a shrug. "I lost, I guess."

"But how?" Marina said. She turned to Hailey. Her eyes looked urgent. "You definitely had her, right? And then . . . something happened. Something changed."

"Yeah, I mean, I *thought* I had her." Hailey laughed. "Well, I had just climbed that colossal volcano and nearly fell into lava—thanks for saving me, by the way. Maybe by the time I fought Golden Jumpsuit, I was more tired than I thought."

"Maybe," Marina said. But she sounded unconvinced.

"Do you have a theory?" Hailey asked.

Marina twisted her hair. "I don't know. Possibly. It seems mad, though."

"Try me!"

"You were unnaturally tired after fighting her. It wasn't a normal energy depletion. And it's certainly not how you act in times of crisis. You always get an adrenaline rush, Hailey. Like how you handled that snake tonight? You are *more* spirited during catastrophe, not less."

"Okay?" Hailey said.

"Maybe . . ." Marina swallowed hard. "Maybe the Mythics are not the only ones with special powers."

Hailey didn't know what to say to that. Marina was right—it *did* seem mad. And impossible. But then again—she looked at Kraken on her right shoulder, who gently squeezed her before scampering back to Marina—until two weeks ago, *this* was impossible.

Maybe nothing was impossible.

And if Marina was right—if the villain had followers and powers—then just how dangerous *was* Golden Jumpsuit?

BERRIES

How they made it through the night was anyone's guess. Perhaps Golden Jumpsuit's head-to-toe ink bath kept her busy. Maybe Ember and Marina's smoke screen had done the trick. Maybe they owed their good fortune to the hundreds of waterfalls in Splashside Falls.

Either way, everyone knew they were on borrowed time. They packed up camp quickly . . . not that there was anything to pack.

"We can't fly," Ember said. "She'll be searching the skies."

"But we can't walk," Marina said. "If she is searching the ground, we'll be too slow. We need familiar-travel."

"We need an eight-armed beast!" Hailey said.

Marina and Kraken bonded. She curled an arm around each Mythic, and Ember shielded Ashley again. They passed through the waterfall.

Hailey squinted from the bright sun. She expected to see the mossy, misty, barren landscape of Splashside Falls. When her eyes finally adjusted, what she saw was a crowd.

There were twenty people or more, wandering all around the falls. Carrying pitchforks.

A search party . . . and not the good kind.

"THERE THEY ARE!" shouted someone Hailey had never ever met.

"Someone call *her*!" roared someone else.

The entire mob turned their way. They began to run toward them from all directions.

"GO, GO, GO!" Hailey shouted as Kit cried, "GET OUT OF HERE, MARINA!"

Marina hiccupped. Then she ran as fast as her wiggly arms could carry her, dodging all types of people and all kinds of familiars. Hailey knew that Marina was not as nimble on land as she was in the water. But a giant monstrous Mythie—even one out of her element—was still better than no Mythie at all. Hailey cheered as Marina jumped, squirted water jets, and summoned a wave to carry the Mythics away. Once the waterfalls became sparse, Marina disappeared inside a patch of trees.

The kraken continued to scuttle quickly across the land, even as the trees became denser. The farther they traveled, the colder the air got and the more the trees started to turn into evergreens.

After a while, the giant kraken began to wheeze. The beast slowed . . . and then stopped. And then— with a pop—Hailey, Ember, Pippa, and Kit dropped to the ground as Marina and Kraken separated.

"Ouch?" Kit said, rubbing her backside.

Marina panted. Kraken splayed her limbs out wide. She was as limp as a gummy worm. "I'm sorry," Marina said. "Do you think—are we safe?"

"Marina, you left those people in the dust ages ago," Pippa said. "You did great."

"But now we're in a dark and dangerous forest of evergreens!" Marina said. "Exposed to the elements, without shelter, sitting ducks for any of Golden Jumpsuit's minions to find us. Or wolves. Or ticks. What if it rains? What if it snows? What if we get lost out here forever?"

Hailey shrugged. "We can always use Ashley to fly out of here—"

"But what if Golden Jumpsuit sees us? What if Golden Jumpsuit has sympathizers who fly too? What if we're never safe, no matter where we go?"

Marina was spiraling.

"It's okay," Pippa said, crawling to Marina and wrapping an arm around her shoulder. "Look, no one is around us. We're alone out here. All we need to do is come up with the next best action. What's one thing we can do right now?"

"I've said it before, and I'll say it again," Kit said. "FOOD."

"And shelter," Ember said. "I can get a fire going?"

"Come on," Pippa said, getting to her feet. She grabbed ahold of Marina's hand and helped her up. "I can help Ember gather firewood. Marina, why don't you go with Kit and search for food?"

"Me too!" Hailey said. She did *not* want to sit around, building shelter. She would so much rather go on nature's treasure hunt. She pointed ahead. "I'll race you! Last one there's got a slug familiar!" Hailey started to bolt. Well, she tried, anyway. Her ankle still felt strange, so it was more like a limp followed by a series of hops on her good foot.

She barely made it to the finish line ahead of Kit and Marina.

"Okay," Hailey said. "First one to pick fifteen

berries wins the prize—"

"Slow down!" Kit said, sounding an awful lot like Hailey's family. "You have to know what you're doing before you forage!"

Hailey sighed deeply as Kit explained the difference between poison berries and regular berries. Kit knew a lot about berries, having grown up in the forest of Woodside Timbers. Marina knew a

lot about berries too, having read about them in a book, and sometimes she chimed in with things she knew.

But this was like *torture* to Hailey. She felt like she was in school all over again, and the whole *point* of being a Mythic was that she got a forever pass to skip school. She just wanted to go adventuring!

At long last, Kit and Marina stopped talking, and Hailey realized she didn't hear or remember anything they said. But it was okay. She could do this alone. After all, how hard was it to collect berries?

They split up to accomplish the task, and at once, Hailey happened upon a bush with goldish-yellow berries. Wait, what did Kit say about the yellow ones again? There was some sort of cutesy rhyme that Hailey struggled to pay attention to. When a berry is yellow, eat it, good fellow? When a berry is gold, it's good to be bold? Something like that.

Well, it looked round and delicious, anyway. Her stomach growled in approval. She was beyond hungry.

She sniffed it. It didn't *smell* poisonous. Not that she knew what poison smelled like.

She licked it. It didn't *taste* poisonous. Not that she knew what poison tasted like.

After a minute of not dropping dead, she decided she was good to go. She plucked a whole bunch of berries off the bush and stuffed them straight into her cheeks.

The yellow berries were *delicious*. An explosion of flavor in her mouth. She ate her fill.

Once her hunger had subsided, Hailey crammed more into her vest pockets. Then she walked back to the meeting spot, eager to share her find with Marina and Kit. *Just wait until they taste these*, Hailey thought as she scratched her neck.

She needed another taste. Her tongue was feeling a little funny, probably from how much she ate after a whole day of barely eating anything. She popped a few more berries in her mouth.

Kit and Marina emerged from opposite sides of

the forest. Kit held a whole bunch of nuts and crimson berries in her shirt. Marina was holding Kraken, and Kraken had blue-colored berries wrapped in each of her eight arms.

"Look what I found!" Hailey said, holding one of the yellow berries between her teeth. She scratched her face. "Cool, right? They're super tasty!"

"Hailey!" Marina cried. "Those are the poison ones!"

WATER VS. FIRE

Hailey spit out the berries immediately.

Kit groaned. "When a berry is gold, leave it to mold! I taught you the rhyme!"

"Oops," Hailey said as her eye started to swell shut. "I forgot!"

"Is she going to die?" Marina cried.

Hailey's face was swollen and splotchy and itchy, but it wasn't nearly as bad as the time she rolled around in poison ivy, or the time she got sprayed by a skunk, or the time she got bitten by fire ants. So, she counted this as a win.

"I'll be thine!" Hailey said as her tongue began to swell.

"Marina!" Kit said, alarmed.

But Marina was already on it—she and Kraken bonded. They carried Hailey in two tentacles, while Kit rode on the kraken's head. They made it back to the campsite with Ember and Pippa, who were standing by a roaring fire. And Ashley, who was flying excitedly around Ember's head.

"Oh, you're back! That was quick. If you found any nuts, we can cook th—" Ember turned around, and the smile slid off her face. "What happened to you, Hailey? You look terrible."

"I've been *poisoned*," Hailey said dramatically. But with her swollen tongue it sounded a lot like gibberish.

"She ate the wrong berries!" Kit explained.

Marina laid Hailey against a tree. Then Marina unbonded with Kraken and leaned over Hailey with a concerned expression.

"Ice!" Kit said. "We need ice! Why can't we find our Mythies in populated towns, with convenience stores and medicine shops? I mean, where are we going to get ice?"

Marina took a deep breath. "We have my water and Ember's fire." Marina squirted a bit of water in Hailey's face, but Hailey was not expecting it. She coughed, which made her rashes burn. "Did that help?" Marina asked.

"No!" Hailey said in a chipper voice. "Leth try fire nexth!"

"No way!" Ember said.

"Yeah, let's definitely *not* blast fire at you," Kit said.

Pippa bent down and held Hailey's hand. If only Pippa could scratch the rash forming on her hands—oh, that would hit the spot!

Kit reached into her pockets and turned them inside out. "I have nothing to help. I lost everything in the sea!"

"We all did." Marina leaned over. "Hailey, can you drink? I think we should try to dilute the berries—wash them through your system."

Pippa and Marina helped her into an upright position, while Kit fetched a water bottle from Marina's backpack. Hailey drank, but with every sip, she felt worse. Her stomach curdled. She had this pit that was getting sharper and sharper—

She leaned forward and threw up.

Kit shrieked and jumped away, which was funny to Hailey considering that was *all* she did on the SS *Seashanty*. Marina recoiled. Pippa held on tight to Hailey's hand.

"How do you feel?" Pippa asked.

"On a scale of one to ten, how likely are you to

hurl again?" Kit said warily.

Hailey grinned. She actually felt a lot better. The rashes were still itchy, and her face was still swollen, but she was pretty sure the poison berries were all over the forest floor.

You win some, you lose some, Hailey thought, and she leaned back against the tree trunk.

Everyone looked at her with a concerned expression. "Maybe we should stay put until Hailey rests up," Ember said.

Hailey tried to protest, but she was too tired. So the other Mythics got to work making camp.

It had been another long day. Hailey wondered if every day on an adventure would be a long one. She never thought being a hero would be so exhausting. Or nauseating. Or itchy.

Her skin was BURNING. Hailey closed her eyes and tried to will the itch away, and

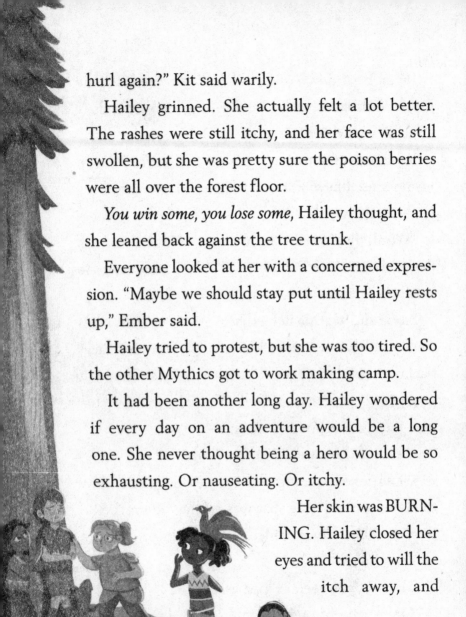

when that didn't work, she scratched and scratched and scratched. But it didn't help—it only made her skin angrier. Her skin stung viciously.

Long after everyone else had eaten and dozed off, long after the fire had dwindled to ashes, Hailey still couldn't sleep.

Talk about a rough day. She could hear her mom and stepdad in her head telling her to slow down. She could hear her big sis Nova's last words to her on the shore of Seaside Sands before they parted ways: *Please don't dive into danger.*

Good thing they couldn't see her now . . .

Hailey was the last to wake up. Marina and Kit were roasting chestnuts for breakfast. Pippa was helping Ember redo her pigtails.

"Good morning, sleepyhead!" Pippa said brightly. "How are you feeling?"

"Better," Hailey said.

"No, better than better! Better than best!"

"You look like your old energetic self," Kit said.

"I think your body needed rest from all that poison," Marina pointed out.

"And now I am READY TO CONQUER THE WORLD! MWAHAHAHA!" Hailey cackled. "But in a *good* way, of course! Not a Golden Jumpsuit way!"

Ember winced as Pippa pulled one of her pigtails a little too tight. "Yes, we'll keep following your arrow, but I think we should make camp earlier than usual so Marina and I can practice with our powers."

Hailey pouted. "But that means it'll take longer to get to my Mythie!"

"I know," Pippa said gently. "But hopefully not that much longer."

"And we could actually be *ready* the next time we have an encounter with Golden Jumpsuit or her underlings," Ember said.

"Tactically, this is what's best for the group,"

Marina said, and Kit nodded in agreement.

Group, schmoop! Hailey thought.

Well, there was no use getting upset about it. She just had to find some way to make this time exciting and fun.

They walked for half the day, and they stopped after lunch. Marina and Ember left to find a clearing of trees to practice in. And Pippa, Kit, and Hailey were *supposed* to be gathering sticks for their eventual campfire.

"NOOOOOOOOOOOOO!" Hailey cried as she dropped the sticks she collected. She was so bored she could scream. She was so bored she *did* scream. "I think we should practice too!"

"With our nonexistent powers?" Kit said.

"We have powers," Hailey said. Hailey picked up the three longest sticks she had collected. One for each of them.

"So, are you going to tell us what these imaginary powers are?" Kit asked. "Because last time I checked,

I can't shoot fire or water out of my hands."

Hailey handed them each a branch. "We're going to practice sword fighting."

"Um, Hailey? We don't have swords, though."

"DEFEND AGAINST ME!" Hailey leaped forward and jabbed the air in front of Pippa. But Pippa just stood there. Hailey shook her head. "No, you're missing the point."

Kit looked at the pointy end of the stick.

"No, not *that* point! This exercise isn't to help you learn sword fighting—not really!"

"Being resourceful! Getting out of scrapes using nothing but your environment! The world around us is full of items that could help us. And our power is BRAINS."

Pippa and Kit looked at each other, and they grinned.

"Now DEFEND AGAINST ME!" Hailey said, charging toward them again. Her branch collided with Pippa's branch. Pippa backed up until she was against a tree. With her non-sword hand, she grabbed the pine needles off the tree and threw them at Hailey, who closed her eyes out of instinct.

"Good," Hailey said, nodding her approval. "That's how you use your environment."

Now for Kit. Hailey whipped around.

"SNEAK ATTACK!"

But Kit was ready. She pelted pine cone after pine cone at Hailey.

"Excellent work!" Hailey praised, ducking behind her hands. "You know—ouch! Pine cones are like extremely hard, extremely pointy snowballs!"

"I never would have thought to throw them," Kit said. "But you're right, Hailey—there are a lot of things in the forest that can be useful."

They took turns being the attackers and the defenders, trying to one-up each other. Hailey had

to admit—her friends were doing a great job. Maybe she didn't give them enough credit.

Still, it was one thing to practice, and another thing to apply it in battle.

Hailey, Pippa, and Kit trained until they were out of breath. Then it was time to check in on Marina and Ember.

They walked to a different clearing—and Hailey saw a battle that put their stick fighting to shame.

Marina and Ember were standing across the way from each other—their Mythies perched on their

shoulders—with fire and water raging between them. Ember sent fireballs Marina's way, and Marina doused them with liquid. Then Marina sent water jets Ember's way, and Ember put up a fire wall.

But Marina was definitely beating Ember. It was only natural, since Marina had had more time to understand her powers.

It was beautiful and amazing, and Hailey could have *died* of impatience watching it. Because how long did she have to wait before she got her own powers? And what powers would she have? Hopefully laser eyes! Or laser hands! Or laser skin! Everything laser!

At last, Ember waved her hand in surrender, and she plopped on the ground. She was panting hard. Hailey ran over to her.

"Ember, that was the SINGULAR COOLEST THING I'VE EVER SEEN."

Ember shook her head. She wiped sweat off her brow. "It wasn't good enough. I can't last very long

with my fire before getting tired and overheated."
Ashley trilled. Then she fanned Ember's face with
her wing. "Ahhh, that feels *so* much better."

"I thought you were AMAZING," Hailey said.

Ember shook her head. "I have to improve. I have
to be able to protect everyone."

Hailey found that amusing because protecting
everyone was totally *her* job. She patted Ember
on the shoulder. "It's okay. You'll keep practicing,
and—"

"You mean that, Hailey?" Ember said. "You'll
let us keep this same schedule
another day?"

"Oh, um . . ." That was
not what Hailey meant.
Wasn't Ember
good enough to
move on with their
jouney—*Hailey's*
journey? How

many more slow-down days could she bear?

Another one, at least. Ember called out excitedly to the others. "Hailey said we can do this again tomorrow! Team player!"

"Hip hip HOORAY!" Pippa cheered.

"Proud of you!" Kit said.

"I think that's so very smart, Hailey," Marina said.

Ugh! If only she said take-backsies!

Now it was too late. They were celebrating her for reasons she didn't understand. And—Hailey knew—for reasons she didn't deserve.

Did they think they'd successfully changed her? Suddenly, she came crashing down. It felt like they collectively clipped her wings when all she wanted to do was fly.

CHILL OUT

They were spending *way* too much time traveling. Even though Hailey's arrow was glowing bright, and even though she was eager to go, no one else seemed to be in a hurry.

She was tired of walking in the evergreen forest. All Hailey wanted was to have the superphoenix fly them to her Mythie. But Ember, Pippa, Kit, and Marina were in agreement that the trees provided more cover from Golden Jumpsuit and her spies. And they weren't walking as far as they had before—because every day, they stopped early so that Marina and Ember could practice their powers.

Hailey patiently—okay, *impatiently*—waited for an opportunity to take-backsies this whole training thing. She thought she'd have her chance once they made it to Mountainside Snows, which was where her arrow seemed to be pointed.

Every day, she knew they were getting closer, because of the temperature drop. And because of the light dusting of snow that appeared in the morning hours.

On the fifth day of morning snowfall, Hailey woke up first. She built the fire as Marina, Pippa, Kit, and Ember shook in their sleep. Hailey's hand was getting brighter—so bright it looked like a star. It was time. She had waited long enough.

And though she *hated* asking for help and preferred to fetch her Mythie alone and come back with the surprise, she knew she needed Ember to fly her there.

"Good morning!" Hailey announced to the group.

The other Mythics stirred. "Wake up! Time to go get my MYTHIE OF MONSTROSITY!"

"Hailey, what time is it?" Kit asked.

"SUNRISE!"

Kit groaned.

"The sun is shining! My arrow is shining! The world is shining! Let's go get my Mythie!"

"We should probably just go collect it," Kit grumbled, "or I might never get sleep again."

"Well?" Ember said. "We seem to be close now. Maybe you're right, Hailey—maybe it *is* time."

"Plus I don't think we can handle any more snows," Marina shivered. "Not in these clothes. Not unless

we want hypothermia."

"Are you excited?" Pippa said, beaming at Hailey.

Excited was an understatement. Hailey was nearly buzzing. She didn't know what exactly her arrow was pointing to or what was coming next, but she had a really good feeling.

After all this waiting, it was *her* turn! Her adventure!

Ember and Ashley melded together. Just like before, the phoenix picked up the others—two girls per claw. This time, Hailey was riding with Pippa, and Kit was sharing a claw with Marina.

"Here we go!" Hailey hollered as they flew higher and higher into the sky.

The climate got colder as they flew, and the tallest evergreens wore jagged icicles. Hailey had the urge to reach out and lick an icicle. But she stopped herself with all the willpower she had. The last time she had encountered an icicle—on a family vacation in Tundraside Frosts—her tongue was stuck to it for

thirty
whole
minutes.
Never again.
For some rea-
son, the temperature didn't
bother Hailey. She was full of adrenaline. But Pippa
shivered beside her.

Hailey wrapped her friend in a big hug. "Here, we
can share my puffer vest, Pip!"

"Aww, thanks, Hailey," Pippa said, snuggling
closer. "I'm not dressed at all for Mountainside
Snows."

Hailey looked down at her palm. Mountainside Snows seemed to be, indeed, where her arrow
was pointing. But not the cute little mountain village with the ice rink and the twinkle lights.
Her arrow was steering them toward
the wild. Where the mountains

loomed tall, and the clouds hung low, and the wind was a sharp, icy slap.

Except all of a sudden, Ember began to descend.

"No, no! What are you doing?" Hailey shouted. "My arrow is pointing—that way!"

But she couldn't get an answer until Ember and Ashley unbonded, after they had landed firmly on the snowy ground on the outskirts of the Mountainside Snows village.

"No detour! No detour!" Hailey chanted.

"Slow down," Ember said, which were two words Hailey was beginning to *hate*. "I'm wearing a tank top. Pippa and Kit are in short sleeves. You're in shorts. None of us is dressed for the weather!"

Hailey sighed. "I thought this was *my* adventure. My turn to call the shots!"

"Yes," Ember said. "But you have to put the group's needs ahead of your own."

"Why?"

"Because we're a team!" Kit said. "I thought you finally understood that."

They walked into the village, and Hailey trudged behind the group. She harrumphed as Ember and Marina went inside a clothing shop with all their money. Why did Hailey always have to slow down? Why was she always hostage to the group?

Hailey paced outside of the store. She wandered to the ice rink. She saw a newspaper stand, and something caught her eye. She picked up a paper.

THE MYTHICS: WHERE ARE THEY NOW?

Join us as we track the Mythics across the world and learn what they're up to.

"If you read it, you're going to have to buy it," said the man working the stand, his ferret familiar wrapped around his neck.

Hailey put the paper down. She walked back to where Kit and Pippa were talking in front of the winter gear store. Then she dragged them to the newspaper stand.

"You really have to buy that," the man said as she picked up the newspaper for a second time.

When Kit and Pippa read the headline, their eyes bulged.

"Well, *that's* going to be a problem," Kit whispered. "Now every one of Golden Jumpsuit's followers will know where to find us."

Pippa hummed. "And Golden Jumpsuit herself."

"Okay, kids, pay up," said the man with the ferret.

"Sorry, no money," Hailey said. "But can you tell us . . . what are those mountains?" She pointed in the direction of her arrow.

He looked at Hailey with curiosity. "That's the tallest peak in Mountainside Snows—Mount Verglas. You're not going to climb it, are you?"

"Maaaaybe," Hailey said.

"But you can't climb Mount Verglas! It's far too dangerous. People freeze up there. You—" He paused. He looked down at the newspaper. Then back up at Hailey, Kit, and Pippa. He squinted.

"You're not . . . are you?"

Every instinct in Hailey's being wanted to introduce herself and her friends as the noble and fearless heroes of Terrafamiliar. But . . . they weren't safe. Not with anyone. Not anywhere. "No," Hailey mumbled. "We wish."

Ember and Marina exited the shop with two bags, and Hailey, Pippa, and Kit ran to meet them. They distributed coats and mittens—the cheapest ones they could get, and they still spent all their money.

Hailey didn't want to admit it, but Mountainside Snows was much more bearable in a puffy coat and warm mittens. But she ripped the right mitten off with her teeth. She needed to see her arrow. It was quite bright, even in the gray overcast sky of Mountainside Snows.

They hid in an alley. Ember and Ashley merged again, and away they flew. Hailey felt bad for Ember that she had to be the one carrying everyone else . . . but only a little. Because Ember was super lucky to have such an awesome Mythie. A *flying* Mythie. Nothing could be better than a phoenix.

And as they soared over the last of Mountainside Snow's villages, Hailey had a thought about her own. "Holy smokes! I know what my Mythie is!"

"Oh? What is it?" Pippa said.

"A polar bear!"

Marina shook her head. "That's not a mythical creature."

"Says the girl who thought her Mythie was a narwhal," Kit teased.

Ember let out a caw that sounded a lot like a laugh.

"Okay," Hailey said. "Well . . . how about a solar bear. A bear made of solar energy and pure light. Or a molar bear! Just think about it. Something tall and scary is coming toward you step by step, inch by inch. Is it a bear? Is it teeth? It's BOTH."

As they flew toward the tallest, northernmost mountains, the air grew even thinner. The clouds became threateningly dark—

Marina whimpered. "Anyone else feel anxious that we're flying into a storm? Just me? Okay."

Hailey flashed her a thumbs-up. "Don't worry, Marina! Blizzards are cool!"

As soon as Hailey said that, as if to prove a point, the wind started furiously throwing ice and snow and hail at Hailey's face. The wind was biting her nose and ears, and the sleet was bitterly painful. Just like that, the blizzard was no longer cool.

Well, it was only cool in the literal sense.

Hailey watched her arrow intensely. Her hand felt like an ice cube, but it was comforting to watch her arrow get brighter and brighter. That must mean they were on the right track. The glow was piercing through the whiteout, pointing straight ahead—

Her arrow rotated.

Now it was pointing behind them.

"Wait, turn around!" Hailey shrieked over the wind. "My arrow is pointing the other way."

Ember turned around, and her arrow swung back.

"Wait, turn around!" Hailey cried.

Ember turned around again, and her arrow swung back.

"Wait, turn around!" Hailey shouted.

"We're just going in one giant circle!" Kit cried. "We're clearly going around it. We need to land!"

Ember dipped down to the ground. It was a bumpy ride.

"Sorry," Ember apologized, looking at Ashley. "Something feels off."

Hailey looked around. They were standing on a mountain shelf, just in front of a peak. The *tallest* peak. So this was Mount Verglas, huh?

Hailey waded through the snow. So, if flying around this peak made her arrow swivel, then . . . "FORWARD MUSH!" Hailey shouted, running toward the summit.

The mountain shelf wrapped all the way around the peak, and the Mythics walked the entire perimeter. It was near impossible to see in the blizzard, and Hailey didn't know what she was looking for. But she'd know when she saw it.

At last, Hailey found a hole in the mountain rock. Like a human-sized tunnel that led into the center.

This was it! Hailey sprinted in, not even looking back to see if her friends had followed.

Inside, she gasped. The mountain was hollow, and inside the tallest peak of the tallest mountain in the tallest area of Terrafamiliar was an enormous iceberg.

Her hand burned hot—hotter than the time she touched the stove (just to see what it would feel like). "Ouch!" Hailey cried, holding her palm.

Her arrow was spinning wildly. She was in the right place, but she didn't see any beast, mythical or otherwise. She saw only an iceberg in the center of the mountain. Was her Mythie a big block of ice?

"What's going on?" Ember shouted as she and the others entered the hollow. "Why did you run ahead? And—whoa!"

Pippa gasped and pressed her pink nose against the iceberg. Hailey did the same, and that's when she saw something unmoving in the ice. A gigantic creature—blue in color, scaly, with big bat wings, a long snout, talons, spikes.

Her Mythie was a superawesometremendous-terrific dragon. This was the best thing in the whole world—the *perfect* familiar for her. More perfect than she could have ever dreamed.

There was just one teensy-weensy problem . . .

The dragon was frozen solid.

BREAKING THE ICE

"GET HER OUT OF THERE!" Hailey cried as she started clawing at the ice with her bare hands. And when that didn't work, she broke off an icicle and started chipping away at the iceberg.

But Ember stepped between Hailey and the iceberg. "Hailey, slow down—"

"No! I can't slow down!" Hailey said. She dropped the icicle. "My *Mythie* is stuck or hurt or frozen or hibernating or dead, and I have to reach her! And you saying slow down isn't going to help!"

"Um," Marina said, "if we could just think logically—"

"I'm not a thinker, I'm a doer!" Hailey snapped, turning around. "You can all stop trying to change me now. It's not going to happen!" There was dead silence, but Hailey didn't care. She continued to chip away at the ice. She pounded, breathless and urgent. Her hands were cold, and she was no closer to her Mythie, but she had to try!

"Stop that—stop for a second!" Ember said, grabbing Hailey's hand. "What do you mean *change* you? We don't want you to change!"

"Seriously!" Kit added. "You have more energy and enthusiasm in your pinkie toe than Ember, Marina, Pippa, and I have in our whole bodies. Combined. I *wish* I could be as confident as you."

"Or as brave," Marina said.

"Hailey, we love you just as you are," Pippa said, putting her hand on Hailey's shoulder.

"No, but

you said . . ." Hailey dropped her icicle and looked around. *"You have to slow down, you can't be a dare-devil—"* she recited.

Marina laughed. "Oh, Hailey! It wasn't about changing *you*. We wanted you to know that you can rely on *us*."

"I think," Ember said, "that you're so used to doing everything alone. But it's not like that anymore. You're part of a team now. Use us."

Maybe it *was* like that. She'd been in such a hurry to protect her friends and save the Mythies and save the world—that she didn't stop to consider that she could trust them. Depend on them. Even—dare she say it—ask them for help.

She had a twisty feeling in her stomach. She really *did* need their help. Getting to her Mythie was one thing she couldn't do on her own. Chipping through this ice would take a millennium.

"I—please, if you could—maybe . . . ," she stammered. This was very new to her, and she did not know how to say it. She finally whispered, "I want your help."

Ember and Ashley ran to the right side of the ice block and started melting it with fire. Marina and Kraken followed her and began to add water to the mix, which boiled in the heat of Ember's fire. Between the burning fire and the piping hot water, they were finally making progress.

Meanwhile, as fruitless as it was, Hailey, Pippa, and Kit were chipping away at the left side. It felt important to be doing something. After all, Hailey was never very good at waiting around.

"I'm coming for you!" Hailey called to her familiar.

The core of the mountain was heating up fast. If Hailey closed her eyes, she could almost imagine that they were still back at Lavaside Rocks.

As the ice block was getting smaller and smaller, different parts of the dragon began to hit the air. First was the claw at the top of her wing, which twitched.

"SHE'S ALIVE!" Hailey cackled. But then, as more of the dragon's wing broke free from the ice, Hailey began to worry. "Ember! Be careful not to get her with your fire!"

"I don't think that'll be a problem," Ember said, wiping sweat off her brow. She looked like she was nearly at her limit, and her fire was coming out in short spurts now. "I just . . . ever since we got up to the top of Mount Verglas, something doesn't feel right. This feels twice as hard as it did when we were training."

Marina, too, looked like her water was nearly at an end. Like a hose that was bent, the water barely dribbled out of her palms.

"We're almost there!" Hailey encouraged, and Ember nodded determinedly.

What was once ice around the dragon became a giant puddle of water. Hailey sloshed

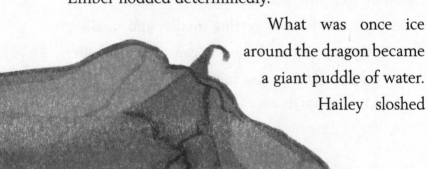

around in it, trying to get to her Mythie. The drag-on's wings were completely free, but her head and torso were still submerged in ice. Just a little more, and her dragon would be free.

CRACK!

The ice around the dragon split in two. The Mythie was snorting and stirring. Out of her nostrils rose vapors—the kind that Hailey could see from her breath right now. For the first time, Hailey was stunned into stillness. Because she couldn't believe how incredible her familiar was—how perfect. How could she *ever* have thought she'd get a kan-garoo? *Of course* she'd pair with a dragon.

Hailey moved forward to bond with her Mythie.

CLANG!

A chain dropped down from the ceiling,

looping around the dragon's neck—leashing her. No, shackling her.

"HEY!" Hailey shouted. She saw a glint of gold against the silvery gray of the mountain rock. The moment she let her guard down? Hailey nearly cursed. "GET OFF MY MYTHIE!"

"I think I'll get *on*," Golden Jumpsuit said smugly.

Hailey ran forward—she knew how this went. All she had to do was get to her dragon before Golden Jumpsuit. Then she could bond with her, thwart Golden Jumpsuit, and finally have the familiar of her dreams.

But Golden Jumpsuit dropped from the ceiling in twice the speed. She landed straight onto the back of the dragon, which roared and thrashed, but Golden Jumpsuit held on tight. She kicked her heels in its sides.

And away Hailey's Mythie flew.

LIZARD IN THE BLIZZARD

Hailey ran out of the mountain and into the storm. The harsh wind threw fistfuls of snow and ice in her face. Her nose froze from the inside out, and every breath she took was like knives—but she didn't care.

Golden Jumpsuit was getting away!

She looked around for anything to use—anything that could help her be resourceful. There was nothing but snow.

"BLAST!" Hailey shouted in frustration.

Hailey's only bit of hope, as she watched her

dragon slip farther away, was that Golden Jumpsuit seemed to have trouble controlling the Mythie.
They rose a few feet, then they flailed back down
again. Golden Jumpsuit pulled tightly on the reins,
but the dragon rebelled against
it. They did loops in the sky,
which was totally unfair
because *Hailey* should be
the one doing loops with
a dragon!

What was happening
up there? Why was Golden
Jumpsuit having so much
trouble with the dragon?
And where was her dragon
going?

"ROAR!" the dragon roared, and
it locked eyes with Hailey—before Hailey's view
was blocked by the storm again.

My Mythie is trying to get to me! Hailey realized.

She had to get to her first. But did she have any way to get up there?

"Do you see her?" Kit yelled, running out of the cave.

Pippa was behind her, drawing the hood on her coat tighter. Marina and Kraken were locked in a tight hug, both of them shivering. And Ember was shielding Ashley, whose flame was very low.

"How can we help?" Pippa said.

That's right. She wasn't alone. She was part of a team.

"Can you fly me up there?" Hailey asked Ember.

"Of course," Ember said, and she merged with Ashley. "Caw!"

Hailey climbed onto a claw, and Ember was off—leaving the other Mythics behind. They fought the wind, rising swiftly, trying to reach Golden Jump-suit. Hailey reached out as far as she could, but the dragon was too far away.

"HOLD ON!" Hailey yelled to her Mythie.

"Ember, can you—" She looked up and gasped. Ember's fire was nearly out. The flames flickered—weak, tiny wisps of what they once were. Her phoenix form, usually alight with molten yellow and orange flames, was now a faint blue color. "EMBER!"

Ember was flying faster now, but something was wrong. The phoenix was gaining speed but losing height.

Hailey looked ahead, keeping her eyes on the dragon. They were close now—close enough to hear Golden Jumpsuit scream, "Cooperate, you filthy beast!" and the dragon snarled in response. Close enough to hear the chains rattle from around the dragon's neck.

Hailey gulped. Could she jump from Ember to her mythical beast? Could she make it before Ember crashed to the ground?

She had to try.

Hailey took the biggest jump of her life. She leaped from Ember's claw, soared through the air, and just narrowly missed the dragon's hide.

She was falling—

She waved her arms wildly.

She caught hold of something cold and metal.

The chain around her dragon's neck! She wrapped her legs and arms around the chain and held tight.

Ember nose-dived to the snow below.

"Ember!" Hailey called. But she couldn't see her

friend in the storm.

She had to save Ember. But she couldn't let go. She needed to climb. If she could just touch the dragon—that's all it would take.

She inched up, but it was easier said than done as the wind slapped her across the face. The storm was trying its hardest to knock her off.

"Oh, no you don't!" Golden Jumpsuit cried, noticing Hailey dangling on the chain underneath the dragon. Golden Jumpsuit tried to get the Mythie to fly upward, but the dragon started wriggling and writhing, moving closer to the ground. Then the dragon did a one-eighty and flew back toward the peak of Mount Verglas.

Suddenly, a jet of water cut through the storm and splashed Hailey in the face. She shivered and looked down. A giant kraken was sending water blasts their way.

"AIM HIGHER!" Hailey shouted, not that Marina could hear her anyway over the raging wind.

Hailey's Mythie flew lower still. Which *should* have made it easier for Marina to splash Golden Jumpsuit off the dragon's back. But something strange was happening with Marina. It took Hailey a moment to see it through the blizzard, but Kraken's arms were dangling limply by her side. It was like Marina was losing energy—and losing it fast.

"COME ON!" Hailey said to herself as she tried to climb the chain. It was wet and cold. She slipped down it. She was dangerously close to falling. "LAND! PLEASE, LAND!" she cried out.

The dragon descended swiftly. Could the dragon hear her? Or were they just perfectly in sync as familiar and human?

"Good monster!" Hailey shouted gleefully as she, the dragon, and Golden Jumpsuit crashed into a powdery hill of snow. They hit it with such force that snow exploded like confetti.

Marina, Kit, and Pippa ran to Hailey.

Golden Jumpsuit groaned as she crawled off the

dragon. She stood between Hailey and her Mythie. And then the villain did something *truly* horrifying.

She pulled out her hand and put it on the dragon's throat. The dragon wailed and whimpered and snorted ice, and her head sagged into the snow.

The same thing was happening to the dragon that had happened to Hailey on the volcano, when she'd touched Golden Jumpsuit. It was a scary trick that Golden Jumpsuit had up her sleeve, but Hailey would not cower.

"This is it, you fiend!" Hailey shouted over the wind. "Surrender! Or meet Marina's water blasts!"

"Um, Hailey?" Marina said, twisting her hair nervously. "About that—something's wrong with my powers. They're not working right. They're . . . well . . ." She sent a water jet flowing out of her hands, but that flow turned into a trickle, and that trickle stopped entirely.

Golden Jumpsuit laughed. "You girls know *nothing*," she said. "Of course your water and the other one's fire aren't working the way they should. Mount Verglas is the farthest point away from the magical epicenter of Terrafamiliar."

"But *your* powers are working!" Kit pointed out.

"I'm special."

The dragon whimpered. Hailey had to do something. No thinking, just doing.

She started to run at Golden Jumpsuit, but the villain chuckled. "I wouldn't do that if I were you." And Golden Jumpsuit squeezed the Mythie's throat tighter—so tight that the dragon twitched. "Poor little Mythics—no leverage and no powers. Whatever will you do?"

"I think we'll manage," said Kit, throwing a giant snowball at Golden Jumpsuit. It pelted the villain right in the face. Golden Jumpsuit took her hand off the dragon's neck to wipe her eyes. Which was just enough of a moment for Pippa to charge in, brandishing an icicle as a sword. And for Kit to run closer, bombarding Golden Jumpsuit with snowball after snowball. "It's not a pine cone, but it'll do!"

Hailey could have cried—they were using her training against the enemy. But Golden Jumpsuit was far too powerful—they'd never beat her with snowballs and an icicle. So what were they doing?

Hailey gasped. It finally clicked! Pippa and Kit were keeping Golden Jumpsuit distracted, giving her the perfect opportunity to sweep in, and—

She touched her dragon's soft underbelly. All at once, Hailey and the dragon began to glow.

THE DAREDEVIL

Hailey felt like freshly chewed gum. She was chomped and gnawed and turned to putty—but then so was her dragon. She reached out for her Mythie in her mind, and she felt the dragon wrap itself around her like a warm hug, even in this icy, frigid blizzard.

At once, she understood—she and her dragon were a team. That was what it meant to have a familiar.

But, unlike everyone else in the world, Hailey knew she had another team too, and they were depending on her.

Hailey's piercingly sharp dragon eyes swiveled toward Golden Jumpsuit. She let out a ferocious roar, spitting cold wind and ice into the air. She pounced forward and bit the fabric of Golden Jumpsuit's golden jumpsuit.

The villain kicked Hailey in the snout and wiggled away from her fangs. Golden Jumpsuit looked frightened for the first time since Hailey had seen her.

Hailey looked to the side. Her teammates were shivering violently.

And suddenly, Hailey understood the coulds and shoulds of the whole situation.

She COULD keep fighting Golden Jumpsuit. She was raring to go. She was a daredevil! The daringest devil to ever daredevil. And she was afraid of nothing. She knew she could do it.

But SHOULD she?

Because her friends were in no shape to fight. Ember was lost somewhere in the snowstorm. Pippa and Kit were out of breath and shaking from the cold. Marina was at the limit with her powers. Meanwhile, Hailey had no idea what her own powers *were*, let alone how long they'd last before she, too, reached her limit. And Hailey still didn't understand Golden Jumpsuit—not enough to beat her completely. The villain said she was *special*, but how? Hailey needed more information. And more preparation. A battle plan.

She couldn't believe she was thinking this, but she shouldn't jump into action right now. She needed to retreat so they could all fight another day.

She waved a wing to her friends. "Hop on!" she said, but it came out as one long "ROOOOAAAAAR!"

Somehow, the Mythics knew what she meant.

Pippa, Marina, and Kit climbed onto Hailey's back, and when they were all holding on to her striking scales, she flapped her wings as fast as she possibly could.

The Mythics left Golden Jumpsuit in the middle of the storm, her face contorted in fury.

Get away! Hailey thought. Away from there. And to Ember.

They searched the snow for Ember. The blizzard was too intense. Nothing, nothing, nothing . . .

"There!" Kit cried.

Hailey swooped down. Ember and Ashley had unbonded, and Ember was holding Ashley tight in the snow. They were both trembling. Marina and Pippa helped them onto the dragon.

Hailey fled as fast as her wings would take her. Sure, the storm roughed her up and threw snow her way, but she let out a strong ice breath to clear a path forward. And she continued soaring through the sky until the storm's wrath lessened—and then let up completely.

And then Mount Verglas was behind them. They were just four girls, one tiny kraken, one little phoenix, and a gargantuan dragon swimming through the clear night sky. Hailey roared . . . just for funsies.

She crossed the southern border of Mountainside Snows and didn't land until they were solidly in the flat, icy desert of Tundraside Frosts. The land here was in perpetual permafrost. Just as cold, just as windy as Mountainside Snows, but with none of the blizzards or summits. And now, in the summertime, wildflowers grew. Hailey had seen them before on a trip with Mom, Stepdad, Nova, and Willow.

She was so close to her home now—Cliffside Ledges. But she knew she couldn't go home again. She only wished she had a pocket-sized family, so that they could see her now. Partially because they'd be proud of her. But mostly because she was a massive ice dragon who could never be grounded again.

Kit, Pippa, Ember, and Marina brushed themselves off, and Hailey felt this strange nagging sensation within her. An uncomfortable tug. She didn't *want* to separate from the dragon, but the feeling grew larger and stronger until she could no longer fight it.

She and the dragon unbonded. And Hailey immediately burst into laughter. "DID YOU SEE ME? NO, SERIOUSLY, DID YOU *SEE* ME? I CAN FLY! I BREATHE ICE!"

"We saw!" Ember said, nuzzling her cheek against Ashley's, and the phoenix chirped happily. Hailey was relieved to see that Ashley's blue wisps were gone and her auburn flames were back. "And more importantly, Hailey, we saw you be a team player."

"Yeah, yeah—whatever. Now look at my awesome powers!" Hailey pushed her hands forward. A gust of wind burst out and flipped Kit's hair into her face. "HOORAY! I have wind powers!"

"It would be *lovely*," Kit said as she smoothed her hair back down again, "if everyone would please

stop practicing their new powers on me!"

"Sorry. I haven't learned how to contr—" Hailey cut off when she saw her palm.

Her arrow was gone! Replaced by a glowing star. Well, that seemed about right for a daring hero. "Wait a second! Where's my dragon?" Hailey combed the ground until she found her Mythie, curled up like a cat under a patch of wildflowers. Hailey scooped her up and cradled the teensy dragon in her arms.

"Awww, she's so cute!" Pippa said, petting the dragon's head while the Mythie playfully snapped at her fingers. "What's her name?"

Hailey grinned. "Introducing Icebreathfangtooth-talonslicewarrior, Queen of the Windstorm."

Kit rolled her eyes, but she was laughing too. "That's kind of a mouthful, Hailey."

"Okay, fine." Hailey pouted. "That will be her *formal* name. But you can call her Sherbet, for short."

"Sherbet!"

Pippa squealed.

Hailey began to walk. She'd been here before, after all, and she knew the way. The other Mythics followed her across a field, through the flowers and the frost, and over a hill. Here it was—town center for Tundraside Frosts. It was a sparse village, just like Mountainside Snows.

Hailey sat on a public picnic table across from the bestest beyond best, most delicious hot chocolate shop there ever was. If only they had any money left! Why'd they have to waste all their coin on these coats anyway? They totally could have survived a blizzard without coats! Hot chocolate would have been worth it.

The Mythics sat with her. Not even knowing what they were missing, being only ten steps away from the world's best hot cocoa.

"We have to talk about Golden Jumpsuit," Marina said thoughtfully.

"She's a thorn in my side," Ember said.

"A thorn in ALL OUR SIDES!" Hailey added, and Sherbet let out a snort.

They hadn't seen the last of Golden Jumpsuit. They knew that. But *how* did she keep finding them? "Are her spies really that good? That they keep her informed of where we are *to the minute?*" Hailey asked. "Or is her familiar a tracking animal? Maybe a dog with a really big nose. Or a tick that's stuck to my ankle!" She checked her ankles. All clear.

"I bet her familiar's a cat," Kit said. "She seems to have nine lives."

"Come to think of it, have you ever seen her with a familiar?" Marina asked.

They all shook their heads.

"So . . . her familiar must be something small," Marina deduced. "Small enough that we wouldn't see it when we fought her."

"Well, I guess that means we can rule out a molar bear," Kit teased. "Phew."

Marina shivered. She pulled the coat tighter

around her. She let a long silence elapse as she twisted her hair nervously. Hailey knew she had something on her mind, but sometimes it was best to let Marina take her time with it. At last, Marina said, "My powers were strange. They were off."

"Weaker," Ember agreed. "I was much better when we were practicing in the woods."

Kit frowned. "Golden Jumpsuit said that we were far away from the epicenter of Terrafamiliar, whatever that means."

"I think," Marina said, "that there's some place where the magic comes from. A place where magic is stronger. And we were far from that place, so our magic was weaker. So, what's the opposite of Mount Verglas? Opposite geographically? Atmospherically? Altitudinally?"

Everyone shrugged.

"But I don't understand—her powers worked!" Hailey said. "Why hers, and not yours?"

"She said she was special," Pippa said.

Marina bit her lip—her deep-in-thought face. "It

was interesting. She didn't deny that she had powers. Only that her powers were *different*."

Pippa looked off dreamily. "I wonder who she is."

"Or what she is," Hailey said.

"Or what she wants," Kit said.

"Or why she has followers," Ember said.

The closer Hailey got to understanding the mysteries of Golden Jumpsuit, the further away she felt. Golden Jumpsuit was like a big giant math problem, and Hailey was never very good at math.

"Excuse me," said a voice they didn't recognize.

They looked toward the end of their table. An elderly woman with a very shaggy sheepdog familiar had approached.

Every Mythic stiffened.

"Can we help you?" Marina asked nervously, and Kraken tensed on her head.

"You girls look . . . very busy. Like you're doing important work, and"—her eyes jumped from Sherbet to Kraken to Ashley—"I thought you could use a hot chocolate."

They stared at the woman as she dug into her pocket. She put bills on the table. Way more than what hot chocolate cost.

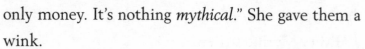

"Ma'am!" Ember said. "It's too much."

"It's very kind of you," Pippa agreed. "But we can't possibly take this."

"You better," the woman said. "I insist. It's only money. It's nothing *mythical*." She gave them a wink.

Hailey could have cried. Instead, she stood up. "You are the NICEST LITTLE OLD LADY I'VE EVER MET—"

"Don't you mention it," the woman said with a blush, "and good luck." She continued on her way.

Marina and Pippa volunteered to get the five hot cocoas from the shop across the street. When they returned, they put two trays down on the wood table, and each of the Mythics took a mug. The drink smelled so deliciously sweet, and it even had mini marshmallows.

The Mythics sipped their hot cocoa. It warmed Hailey all the way down to her tummy.

"There are good people in this world," Pippa said. "It's important to remember."

They nodded.

"It's funny," Ember said. "I think ever since we found out that Golden Jumpsuit has supporters, we've been running from everyone. We haven't known who to trust."

"I think we need to put our faith in people," Pippa said. "Golden Jumpsuit has allies, but I bet we have some too. And we'll never know who they are if we keep avoiding everyone. Maybe we should stop running."

Kit swirled her mug around. "Not *all* the time, though. Like . . . if we encounter someone trying to trap us with a violent bear and a thirty-foot anaconda? Then I think it's okay to run."

"No, that's when we fight!" Hailey said.

"No, that's when you *bite*," Kit teased.

They laughed and sipped their hot chocolate. Hailey was savoring every last drop.

Marina frowned. "Saving the world is still so hard to wrap my head around. Because we don't know what Golden Jumpsuit is up to, or what she wants with our Mythies," she said. "And since we don't know her true motive and goals, we're always one step behind her. Always reacting. When we *should* be predicting her movements."

"Still," Ember said. "Even if we don't know her exact plan, we have to stop her."

That's what Hailey had been saying all along! They had to stop Golden Jumpsuit in her tracks. It was a Mythic's sworn duty to thwart any—and all—villainous fiends that crossed their path. But Hailey finally understood the one word that had been missing every time she expressed that feeling in the past.

"Together?" Hailey said, raising her mug in a toast.

In solidarity, Marina, Pippa, Ember, and Kit clanked their mugs against hers. "Together," they agreed.